What's in Oscar's Trash Can?

and Other Good-Night Stories

By Michaela Muntean

Illustrated by Tom Cooke

On *Sesame Street,* Luis is played by Emilio Delgado

A SESAME STREET / GOLDEN PRESS BOOK

Published by Western Publishing Company, Inc., Racine, Wisconsin 53404

MCMXCII

WHAT'S IN OSCAR'S TRASH CAN?

"Whew! Is it ever hot!" said Elmo.

"Let's go get an ice-cream cone," said Ernie. "Maybe that will help us cool off." Elmo thought that was a great idea, so they headed toward Hooper's Store.

As they passed Oscar's can they noticed a sign.

"'GROUCH REUNION,'" Ernie read.

"What a day for a reunion!" said Elmo. "I'll bet those grouches are even grouchier than usual on a hot day like this."

Just then they heard the rattle of the trash-can lid, and up popped Oscar.

"Brrr," he said. "The water in that swimming pool is chilly. I need to warm up a bit."

"Pool?" asked Elmo. "What pool?"

"*My* pool, of course," said Oscar. "Whose swimming pool do you think I'm talking about?"

"Gee, Oscar," said Ernie, "I never even knew you *had* a swimming pool."

"We grouches are full of surprises," Oscar said, chuckling. "Heh-heh. You should see Uncle Oswaldo and Filthomena! They had a big water fight, and both of them are soaked! Then Fluffy the elephant got in the act and sprayed Grundgetta with his trunk. It was great!"

"An elephant?" cried Elmo. "You mean an *elephant* lives down there with you?"

"Sure," Oscar said with a shrug.

"What else is in your can, Oscar?" asked Ernie.

"Do you mean besides the ice-skating rink?" Oscar asked.

"Ice-skating rink?" Elmo cried.

"Yep." Oscar nodded. "And that reminds me. Slimey's been practicing making figure eights all week. He's going to put on a show, and I don't want to miss it! After that we're going to have a picnic. I'm serving stinkweed coleslaw, burnt potato chips, and hot dogs smothered with sardines."

   "Yucch," said Elmo, but Ernie quickly said, "Gee, Oscar, that
sounds pretty good, especially if we could go swimming first. Say,
would you mind if we came to your reunion?"
   "Mind? Of course I'd mind!" Oscar cried. "We're having a
grouch reunion, and as far as I know, neither one of you is a
grouch."
   "We *could* be," said Elmo.

Oscar frowned and pulled out a mirror. He held it up to Elmo
and said, "Take a look and tell me what you see."

Elmo looked at his reflection in the mirror. "I see one cute
little red monster," he said.

Oscar held up the mirror for Ernie. "Do you see a grumpy face
with thick, scowly eyebrows?"

"No," Ernie admitted.

"Well, that proves it," Oscar said. "Neither one of you is a real
grouch."

Then from the depths of the trash can they heard angry voices shouting and arguing.

"Heh-heh," laughed Oscar. "They're fighting over who gets to bowl first. There's nothing like a grouch reunion to bring out the worst in everyone! I certainly don't want to miss a good argument. So long, and have a really hot, rotten day!"

And with a crash of the trash-can lid, he was gone.

Elmo scratched his head and looked at Ernie. "Do you really think that Oscar has a bowling alley in his can?" he asked.

Slowly Ernie lifted up the edge of the lid and peeked inside the trash can. "I can't see anything," he said with a shrug. "Let's go get that ice-cream cone."

As they walked away they heard loud rumbling. They stopped to look at each other.

"Doesn't that *sound* like bowling, Ernie?" asked Elmo.

"Nah," said Ernie. "It *couldn't* be. Could it?"

BERT'S BIRTHDAY

The first thing Bert saw when he opened his eyes was Ernie staring at him.

"Gee, Bert, it's about time you woke up!" Ernie said. "Let me be the first to wish you a happy birthday, old buddy!"

Bert sat up in bed and looked at the clock. "But, Ernie," he groaned, "of course you're the first! It's six o'clock in the morning!"

"I thought you'd want to get an early start on celebrating," Ernie said. "Just wait until you hear what I've planned for today."

"I can hardly wait," Bert grumbled as he climbed out of bed and put on his bathrobe and slippers.

"I'll be waiting in the kitchen for you," Ernie said as Bert shuffled off toward the bathroom.

While Bert brushed his teeth and got dressed, Ernie set the table. He was all ready when Bert walked into the kitchen.

"Notice anything special about what we're having for breakfast?" Ernie asked.

Bert looked at the bowl of blueberries, the glass of buttermilk, and the slices of banana bread. But before he could answer, Ernie said, "Do you get it, Bert? Everything starts with the letter *B*! That's because today is your birthday, Bert, and both *birthday* and *Bert* start with the letter *B*. Did you ever think about that, Bert?"

"Not really, Ernie," Bert answered.

"That's why you've got me for a friend, old buddy," Ernie said. "I'm here to think of these things for you. We're going to have a whole *day* filled with the letter *B*!"

Bert smiled and buttered a piece of banana bread. "You know, Ernie, now that I'm awake, I'm beginning to think it's a good idea. What are we going to do?"

"Gee, Bert, I'm glad you asked, because we have to get going right now. Come on!" Ernie cried, and he led the way down the stairs to Sesame Street. They reached the bus stop just as a big blue bus pulled up.

"Where are we going?" Bert asked when they had found seats.

Ernie smiled. "It's a surprise," he said.

After a while Ernie said, "We get off at the next stop."

When they got off the bus, Bert said, "Ernie, this is my favorite beach!"

"I know, Bert," said Ernie. "Remember, this is B-day, and *beach* starts with the letter *B*. And look, I remembered to bring your bathing suit, a beach ball, our toy boats, and a badminton set."

All morning Ernie and Bert played on the beach. When it was time for lunch, Ernie opened a big basket. "I brought baloney sandwiches, two bottles of Burpee soda, a three-bean salad, and brownies."

"Why, everything starts with the letter *B*," Bert said.

"Now you're getting the idea," Ernie said.

After lunch Bert said, "This has been a great day, Ernie. Thanks."

"It's not over yet," said Ernie. "In fact, this is just the beginning. Come on, we've got to get back home."

When the bus stopped at 123 Sesame Street, Ernie hurried up the stairs, and Bert followed.

"Ta-da!" Ernie cried as he opened the door. There stood all of their friends, singing "Happy birthday, Bert." Balloons hung from the ceiling, and boxes were piled on the table.

All of Bert's presents started with the letter *B,* too. Grover gave him a bird book. Big Bird had baked him a batch of birdseed cookies. The Count gave him a box filled with bottle caps. Elmo gave him a brick with the letter *B* painted on it. "It's a paperweight," Elmo explained.

That night, when everyone had gone home, Bert said, "Thank you, Ernie. That was the best birthday I've ever had."

"Really, Bert?"

"You *bet*," said Bert. "It was *beautiful, brilliant,* and a real *blast.*"

THE END OF THE DAY
By Ernie

Sometimes, at the end of the day, I like to sit quietly on the front stoop. My shadow stretches out in front of me, but because of the steps, it has crinkles in it like the folds in an accordion.

Soon the streetlights come on, and I can see tiny bugs flying around them. I wonder if the bugs were there all the time, and I couldn't see them because there weren't any lights. Or did they fly over when the lights came on? There's time to think about these things when you sit on the stoop at the end of the day.

I hear mothers and fathers calling to their children to stop playing and come inside.

"El-mo," calls Elmo's mother, and her voice trails off like a train whistle.

"Nick!" calls Nick's father, and his voice is quick and sharp, like a dog's bark.

"Mar-eee-anne," calls another mother, and it sounds like she is singing a song. I hope Mary Anne doesn't go in right away so I can hear her mother call her again.

Another thing I hear is Prairie Dawn practicing the piano. On Mondays, when she is learning a new song, she plays slowly and makes a lot of mistakes. But by Friday she can play the song all the way through without any mistakes at all.

I see Luis turn out the lights in the Fix-It Shop. He turns over the OPEN sign so that now it says CLOSED. He locks the door. I wonder if he got everything fixed today. When he sees me sitting on the stoop, he waves, and I wave back.

As the sun creeps down behind the tall buildings up the street, I begin to feel cool. Now it's time for all the people on the other side of the world to have *their* turn with the sun. I put my head back and look straight up at the sky. When I see the first star of the evening, I close my eyes tight and make a wish. When I open my eyes again, there is another star. And another and then another. Soon there are so many stars that I can't count them.

Now it is dark and time to go inside. As I climb the steps I think about how nice it is to sit on the front stoop at the end of the day.